TENTACLES WITH BENEFITS

CONNOR CROWE

FATED FIRE FOUNDRY

A free tale from the world of Nox Bay is all yours!

Felix, formerly a professional thief, is adjusting to his new life in pack lands. But when he receives a mysterious riddle and his mate goes missing, Felix must use his skills once more. Join him and the rest of your Nox Bay friends as he uncovers new treasures, new locations, and at the end of it all, a sweet moment with his forever mate.

https://dl.bookfunnel.com/pey6si01dd

Join my Facebook group Connor's Coven for live streams, giveaways, and sneak peeks. It's the most fun you can have without being arrested ;)

https://www.facebook.com/groups/connorscoven/

Darkvale Dragons

One Knotty Night (free)

The Dragon's Runaway Omega

The Dragon's Second-Chance Omega

The Dragon's Forbidden Omega

Dragon's Feast (free short story)

Darkvale Dragons Books 1-3 Box Set

Dorvakian Legends (with Crista Crown)

Prince's Gambit

Love in Diamond Falls

Summer Heat (free prequel)

Ruby Heat

Topaz Heat

Vale Valley (multi-author series)

Mated Under The Mistletoe

That Magical Moment

Nox Bay Pack

Stealing His Heart

The Crimson Fox (free short story)

Protecting His Heart

Claiming His Heart

Sharing His Heart

TENTACLES WITH BENEFITS

A man's gotta do what a man's gotta do.

In my case, that meant picking up a job as a night watchman at the local aquarium. It didn't pay much, but it was better than nothing. Especially since I'd struck out on every other listing in town. What did I have to lose?

Well, besides my apartment, my bike, not to mention my dignity...

"Requirements?" I asked the man on the phone, a Mr. Collins that was the only thing left standing between me and a paycheck. "What requirements? It's just a night watch position, right? All I gotta do is sit there, maybe make a couple rounds, make sure no one's up to no good."

Mr. Collins coughed nervously. "Yes, yes, of course. We've a few new specimens in our collection that are still getting acclimated to the tanks here." He paused for a moment, and I could have sworn I heard something dripping. "If you hear something beating on the glass, don't be alarmed. It's quite normal as they adapt to their new surroundings."

Well, that wasn't foreboding at all. Just what kind of "new specimens" were they talking about? Still, it wasn't like I had any other choice.

"Okay." I huffed. "I'll be the best night watchman you've ever had." *Just hire me. Please.*

The line hung silent for a moment longer, then cut to harsh, high-pitched static. I yanked the phone away from my ear, wincing. What the heck was that? Did I lose reception or something? I was about to hang up when I heard a voice come back on the line, saying those two magical words.

"You're hired, kid. Show up at 8 p.m. tonight and not a moment later. I'll know if you do."

Click.

Ooookay then. That was definitely more than a little weird. But I couldn't dwell on it too much. I had a job!

———

I CHECKED MY WATCH. 7:55. I'd brought along a flashlight, a peanut butter sandwich, and a bottle of water with me. I tossed a paperback in my bag as well. Who knew how boring it was gonna be in the dark aquarium all night?

I tried to peer through the darkened glass, but I couldn't see anyone in there. I tried the handle -- locked. How was I supposed to get in there to do my job if the doors were locked? They hadn't exactly set me up with a key...or anything for that matter.

A small red flag leapt up in the back of my mind, but I pushed it aside. Probably just a mistake or a miscommunication. I pulled out my phone and checked to see if I had any messages or missed calls. The dull, empty "no signal" icon flashed up on the screen.

Great.

I wrapped my coat tighter around me as a cold breeze whipped through the air. When I let out a breath, it came out as a puff of steam. *Where was he?*

I turned around and was about to head back to my bike when I heard the lock rattle and the door open. "Oh, there you are! Come on in, get out of the cold."

Mr. Collins waved me inside and I followed his lead, discarding my coat on a hanger in a side room. Where the outside world howled with wind and rumbled with the hint of an oncoming storm, the inside of the aquarium was pleasant and still, filled with soft splashes of water and the faintest scent of glass cleaner.

"Let me just take a moment to show you around. If you'll follow me..."

The aquarium had always been a lovely, peaceful place. I'd spent many days here as a child, watching the fish glide easily through the water and wondering what it must be like.

Unfortunately, the cold reality of adult life had set in and I was no longer the innocent child looking on in joy. I had overdue rent, a streak of bad luck finding a job, and a pile of unpaid bills growing on my kitchen counter.

I sighed. Why did everything have to cost money?

"And that's just about it," Mr. Collins finished. I realized then that I had spaced out during the whole tour. *Way to go, Evan.* "Do you have any questions for me?"

Did I ever. Instead, I gave him a smile and a nod, shaking his hand. "Thanks a lot, Mr. Collins."

"Please," he insisted. "Call me Harv."

"Harv," I repeated.

"Well, good luck!" He headed for the door and gave me a wave. "If you run into any trouble, the numbers to call are there in the staff room. The keyring's also there, though we should be all locked up for the night. See ya in the morning and give me a call if you need anything!"

With that, he was out the door...and I was alone.

I never realized how quiet the aquarium got at night. Every other time I'd been here, there were school groups, tourists, staff, and custodians all bustling about. Not to mention the screaming children, the old grandmas in wheelchairs, and the occasional dog (some people paid no attention to pet restrictions).

But now...the aquarium was dark. Silent. Just me and the fishes.

It sent a chill down my spine to think about, though I couldn't have said why. I didn't have any problems spending time alone. Hell, I'd done it my whole life. Let's just say I was never the most socially gifted guy, and I'd grown up an only child to two absent parents.

Solitude was basically a way of life by this point. Not that I wouldn't mind some company...

I shook the thought away and got up from the desk Collins planted me at. Oh, sorry-- *Harv*. Even the name made my skin crawl. There was something *off* about that guy, but as long as he paid me, I couldn't complain. Much.

It was time for my first set of rounds, so I grabbed the flashlight, the keyring, and set off through the maze of hallways. There wasn't much to see--I mean, much out of the ordinary. I stopped by each exhibit for a few minutes, just taking in the calm beauty of the aquatic life. How serene must it be to glide amongst the waves. How freeing, to swim anywhere you pleased with the flick of a fin.

I envied them.

In reality they were the ones confined in these glass cages, but in my own life I felt like I was the trapped one. I sunk down on one of the benches and watched as a school of clownfish sailed by. They had friends. They had a whole school of buddies to back them up. What did I have?

A shitty shoebox of an apartment, a beat-up old bicycle, and a neighbor that smelled constantly like weed. Yup, living the dream.

I rolled my eyes.

Dating? Forget about it. I'd had a couple casual fucks, but I always left feeling even more empty than before. I couldn't put my finger on what, but they were just *missing* something. So I stayed out of it. No need to waste either of our time when I knew it wasn't gonna go anywhere.

A noise took me out of my longing thoughts. Strangely familiar. Then it came to me: that was the same mysterious noise I'd heard when on the phone with Harv. It came again, this time clearer. Closer.

I leapt up and flicked on my flashlight. *First night on the job, and already some action.* Sweeping it around, I searched for the source of the sound, but found nothing. The high ceilings and glass tanks echoed everything.

Was this what Harv was talking about? I wondered. He'd talked about some new "acquisitions" causing a bit of noise, but I hadn't thought much of it. Still, it was my job to investigate. I left the huge viewing room and crept down a hallway. I swung the flashlight left and right, still on my guard. My heart beat just a little bit faster, my breaths a little shorter.

But anxiety and adrenaline wasn't the only thing I was feeling. The closer I got, the hotter I felt. I tugged at my collar and wiped at my forehead. Since when did it get so hot in here? I checked the nearest thermostat. No change.

That didn't make any sense, but I sighed and pressed on when the noise came again. There was *definitely* something in here. And, much as I didn't want to admit it, that strange heat affected me in all the worst ways.

Not only was I burning up, my cock decided now was a good time to come out and play. Talk about bad timing. I knew I'd just been worrying if I'd ever find a good lay, but seriously...

Focus, Evan. I shook myself and carried on, knowing how bad it'd look if I screwed up this job too. *No pun intended.* Unfortunately, the more I tried to ignore it, the more naughty thoughts spilled into my brain and clouded everything else. My whole body throbbed with inexplicable need, leaving me powerless to resist it.

I hissed in a breath through gritted teeth and leaned against the wall for a moment to steel myself. This was ridiculous. Totally ridiculous. I was losing it for sure this time. I'd been watching too much porn lately--that had to be it. *And too many monster movies,* I thought with a laugh.

I was a young, horny bachelor. What did you expect?

With that thought still lingering in the back of my mind, I turned a corner and reached the lab and storage rooms. No one ever came back here except for staff when they were prepping new exhibits or restocking supplies. The closer I got, the louder the sound became, though.

Yup, it was definitely back here. But where?

As if on cue, a dim, flickering light spilled out from one of the closed doors. Naturally, the one that said "do not enter."

Because of course, the one place I wasn't supposed to go was the room I needed to investigate. I took a deep breath and stepped closer, holding my flashlight out in front of me like a weapon. There was something almost...soothing about that light beyond the doorway. It ebbed and flowed in a wavy pattern, almost like the ocean. I found myself drawing closer still, watching the waves until I was right against the door.

"Here goes nothing," I muttered to myself, and turned the knob.

I'd never been in this part of the aquarium--and for good reason. The room was larger than I expected, set up with bizarre looking machines and flashing lights. But the real draw dominated the center of the room: a huge, cylindrical tank. Wires and tubes connected it to the nearby machinery, which let off a series of rhythmic beeps. Reminded me of those trackers that they have in hospitals, meant to track heart rate and oxygenation.

But this was no hospital.

The floor had drains every few feet and the rest of it was smooth stone. A far cry from the carpeted walkways that lined the viewing tanks, that was for sure. The floors were wet and slick with water, though from where I couldn't tell. Was the tank leaking? Maybe that's why they'd installed the drains.

I took careful steps toward the center of the room, doing my best not to fall. My heart leapt into double-time and the pounding heat only grew more intense, but I couldn't stop now. A million thoughts and questions wormed their way through my head with zero answers. What was this place? Why was it closed off to the rest of the aquarium?

And why was the mysterious noise--no, the mysterious *force*--coming from within?

I pressed a hand to the glass and leaned in. An overhead light hung above the tank and illuminated the water below, but I couldn't see anything in there. Seemed empty to me. I squinted and pressed my face closer, right up to the glass.

The slow, thudding sound began again, this time so close it echoed through my bones. The glass shivered against my hands.

In a slew of rising bubbles, something appeared. Two hands, pressed up against the glass against mine. And oh God, a face looking right at me!

"Shit!" I yelped and tumbled backward, landing hard on the wet stone floor.

There was a guy in there!

I scrambled to my feet and rushed to the control panel, looking for some kind of emergency release. How had someone even gotten in there in the first place? I had no idea, but I couldn't let the man drown. I did what anyone would do in the situation--I sprung into action, pushed the panic down deep, and hoped I could save his life.

What did all these buttons and dials do? Suddenly I was in some kind of mad science lab instead of a small town aquarium. That disturbing thought aside, I scanned the console till I found a release switch. Someone had taped over it, but I acted on instinct at this point. I ripped it off and pulled the lever, hoping I wasn't too late.

The tank hissed and water rushed out. Thank goodness for the all the drains in the floor, I realized. The machines went haywire, beeping even louder, but all I cared about was that man in the tank. He flailed around in a panic as the water drained away, and maybe I was just seeing things but I could have sworn I saw fins.

Or tentacles.

I gulped at that unbidden thought. Yup, I was 100% going crazy. No doubt about it. Especially since that thought excited me way more than it should.

Way to go, Evan. Even when there's a man in danger, you gotta be thirsty.

The tank drained at last and a hatch hissed open. I crouched down to peer inside and my eyes grew wide.

That was no man.

Not completely, anyway.

The creature in the tank looked to be some kind of fish-man hybrid. Something that couldn't—shouldn't—exist. Just in movies, right? Just in stories.

Just in your dreams.

Faint scales lined his skin and gave off an iridescent sheen. He sported a human enough face and torso (once you looked past the scales), but once you got below the belt, it was a different matter altogether. His lower half was like an octopus, full of long, squirming tentacles. They wriggled around so much I couldn't count them, but there was definitely more than eight.

On top of it all, the man—the creature—was staring right at me with huge, glittering eyes the color of the ocean at midnight. Whatever this thing was, the emotion on its face was clear.

The poor thing was terrified.

And that, more than the startling discovery, spoke to my humanity. I had no idea what this thing was or if it was dangerous, but there was something undeniably intriguing in that glossy black gaze. I reached out a shaking hand and pressed it against the glass. "Hey," I said softly. "Are you okay? Can you hear me?"

I didn't expect much. After all, I was talking to some kind of mutant in a secret lab that shouldn't exist. What were the chances it could understand me at all?

The creature slithered closer and nodded his head slowly up and down. No sounds came out, but the nod was enough. Another thought came then, and with it another one-two punch of guilt.

Crap, if this thing was a fish and not a human, maybe I actually was drowning it. Only this time with oxygen instead of water.

"Do you, um, need water?" I tried to put the words together as simply as I could, praying that he'd get the message.

The same slow head bob. Back and forth this time. No.

He uncurled one of those long, violet tentacles and pointed it at the door I'd come through. The same door warning not to enter.

"What's wrong?" I wondered aloud. "Who put you in here?"

I didn't need him to answer to form a theory about that one. It must have been the supervisor, Mr. Collins. No wonder he was so nervous on the phone. No wonder he was in such a hurry to hire someone, and no wonder he barely told me anything at all before leaving me here for the night.

I watched in awe at the graceful movements of his tentacles, all the way up to the hard lines of his torso, shoulders, and arms. He had sandy, sun-bleached hair that hung in loose curls down to his ears and his curious eyes still watched my every move.

Who would keep such a beautiful, fascinating creature trapped like this?

He slithered toward the opening and I backed up to give him space. He crawled out of the hatch and onto the lab floor, gliding across the room like a snail. Despite my earlier worry about him needing water to survive, he didn't seem to be in any pain. A child's curiosity took its place as he explored the room, poking and prodding at each object in his reach. He looked back to me often, as if waiting for my reaction.

I couldn't blame him for being curious or even a little scared. I felt pretty much the same way. My heart was racing too, and I'd never seen anything like this. Never even *thought* I'd see anything like this with my own eyes.

Was it a mutant? A totally new species? Some kind of secret experiment? I didn't know, but that feeling of heat and connection I'd felt earlier only intensified when I was around him. As crazy as all of this seemed, I wanted to know more about this strange new creature. I wanted to see what was behind those shining black eyes. I wanted to find out where he came from, what he was, and what he wanted.

In the back of my mind, though I didn't want to admit it, I wanted to draw him into my arms. I wanted to hold him and soothe him. He was lost, a stranger in a new world. I knew how tough that could be—I was always a loner myself. Maybe I saw a little bit of myself in him. Maybe I didn't want him to feel the same pain I had.

"Can you hear me?" I asked again. I followed him to the back of the room where piles of paperwork stacked on an old wooden desk. I knew I should do something. I should probably sound the alarm or call for help or try to get him back into the tank, but I couldn't. That intense longing, that feeling of connection in my heart and soul, hadn't gone away. It was coming from him. My hands stopped shaking, but my heart was no less excited. Not to mention my, um, other parts...

This was insane. I remembered learning about animals that put off certain pheromones as mating signals or to warn off predators, but nothing that could affect humans like this.

If this got out, it would be the scientific find of the century. And that was the trouble, wasn't it? Humanity had never seen anything like this before. And humanity, if nothing else, was curious—often to the point of destruction. The creature was trapped in that tank, after all. Was hooked up to all sorts of sensors amid piles of research. Who knew where they'd found him or what they were doing to him. If word got out about this find, every government in the world would be knocking down our door.

The creature slithered over the pile of papers and started picking through them. His hands were agile enough, even had opposable thumbs like we did. I had no idea if he could read at all, but he seemed to know what he was looking for.

Finally he pulled out a manila folder amongst the rest and wrapped it in his tentacles before turning back to me.

"What...what's your name?" I blurted out. It was a ridiculous question, and only one of the millions of unsolved problems. Even if he *could* understand me, how would he answer a question like that?

The long, purple tentacle wrapped around the folder uncurled and thrust the papers toward me. I picked up the packet of paper and stared at the print.

Project Kairius.

I looked up at him. "Is that your name? Kairius?"

He bowed his head.

Okay. Next question. "Where did you come from?" I flipped through the report hoping to find that answer as well, but all I saw were a bunch of charts and numbers that didn't make any sense.

Kairius—or at least, I thought that was his name—curled a tentacle toward me in a come hither motion. I gulped and weighed my options. No one else was here. My phone was dead. If he wanted to kill me, he could. Easily. No one would be the wiser till it was too late.

But when I saw the terror in his eyes, or watched his smooth, curious movements around the lab, I didn't see a predator. I saw someone lost. Someone alone.

I gulped and took a tentative step toward him. All kinds of warning bells went off in my brain, but just as strong was the almost otherworldly force pulling us together. I couldn't explain how, but I *needed* to know more about him.

Just as much as I *needed* relief from this surge of painful, overwhelming arousal.

I took another step, holding my breath and bracing myself for any sudden movements. I kept the path to the exit in my line of sight, just in case, but I crept forward. One more step. Then another.

Just like that, we were face to face. I'd been so panicked I hadn't had a real chance to look at him, but now that he was right in front of me, I noticed the little things.

The dimples in his cheeks. The damp curls plastered across his high forehead. The bobbing Adam's apple on his neck.

The sheen of iridescent scales all the way down his face, arms, and chest was barely noticeable. In the right light, you wouldn't be able to see them at all. His face remained disarmingly human, save for the eyes. He didn't have eyebrows or facial hair—only a few curls atop his head. I wondered for a brief moment why sea creatures needed hair, but then my eye caught something else.

The scales around his navel flattened and lengthened, giving way to a glossy deep purple. The tentacles—ten of them, I counted—were about as long as he was tall, and covered with circular suckers for grip. He moved each of them independently, curling the tips of them toward me in an invitation.

I stood there, rooted to the spot. To stay or to go? To flee or to find out the secret history of a creature no man had seen before?

I took a deep breath, closed my eyes, and stood my ground. He wouldn't hurt me. He wouldn't. I just wanted to talk. To understand. My hand moved without thinking, reaching toward him. I sucked in a breath and traveled the last few inches to touch his skin.

"Oh," I breathed. He was warmer than I'd expected—though to be honest, I don't know what I expected—and I could feel the pulse of life underneath his skin.

Kairius didn't draw away or launch into a murderous rage, so I took that as a good sign.

He fixed me with those searching eyes, though, and I knew he had a message for me.

"What are you?" I muttered under my breath. "How did you get here?"

As if in answer, Kairius reached out to me. His slightly webbed hand found purchase on my shoulder, and before I knew what was happening, the world dissolved around me.

———

THE LAB and the aquarium melted away along with everything I knew. Hallucinations danced around me, more real than any dream. All the while, Kai's hand rested on my shoulder.

Was this...his world?

Spires of bone and coral shot up around me. Flicking, flowing slants of light cut through the waves. Schools of fish swam this way and that, swaying like the sea grass.

Oh my God, I was underwater!

I opened my mouth and clawed at my throat in a moment of panic. Kai was there, though. His touch anchored me. Soothed me. I dragged in a shaky breath. Then another.

This wasn't real. This was just an illusion. A dream. His way of communicating, perhaps.

Fish, coral, and algae surrounded me and dragged me deeper. Salt water rushed against my skin. Bubbles tickled toward the surface. There was more than just a microcosm down here. No, I realized as I looked on in awe, it was something else entirely.

A civilization.

Glittering glass castles reflected the sunlight from above, shooting prisms of light through the endless current. Bright pink and white shells lined the sea floor in such an organized pattern it could have been called a road. Fences of bone led up to the nearest castle, and there I saw them.

There were *more*.

Half-man hybrids floated through the city everywhere I looked. Little ones. Big ones. All different color tentacles, too. The sight triggered some kind of bizarre deja vu, but I'd never seen anything like this before. Not even in my dreams.

Then why did it feel like I *knew* this place? And why did my soul fill with longing for something I'd never had?

The scene changed before my eyes. The utopia became a nightmare in a matter of seconds. Once peaceful creatures fled in terror, leaving everything behind. Turbulent currents rushed past me, and storms of bubbles flew upward to the surface.

The once great city of bone and coral and glass...was collapsing.

Massive spires caved in on one another, crashing soundlessly to the sea floor while its people died. One after another, their life forces snuffed out, crushed by the weight of the wreckage or the ominous black ink spreading in all directions.

It all flashed before my eyes in a matter of seconds, but every feeling hit me right in the heart. The fear. The pain. The loss. The grief. What had happened to these people? What cataclysmic event forced them from their homes and families? And what unnerved me most of all was one ringing word above all else:

Atlantis.

A shock like lightning ripped through my body and I jerked out of the trance. The cold, sterile lab returned. Water seeped through my jeans. My knees scraped against the metal drains on the floor.

And Kai was still next to me.

I scrambled to my feet and away from him as quick as possible, my body on full alert now. "No freaking way," I panted. "This isn't happening. You can't be real!"

My back slammed against the cold metal door and I clawed for the handle. Forget fighting—full flight mode overtook every thought and sense I had, and the only imperative left was to *escape.*

"What do you want from us?" I wailed. "What are you doing here?"

There was no such thing as Atlantis. There was no such thing as tentacle monsters. There was no. Such. Thing!

I twisted the knob at last and took off at a run. Forget this job. Forget this whole place!

I turned a corner so fast I nearly skidded on the polished floors and ducked into the nearest bathroom. The lights clicked on.

Bracing myself against the door, I tried to control my breathing.

"Okay," I repeated to myself. "Breathe, Evan. Breathe." I staggered over to the sink and splashed cold water on my face, grateful for the chill. It took me out of myself for just long enough to forget everything.

Not nearly long enough. My cock pressed up against the counter and strained against my pants, desperate for freedom. I growled and adjusted myself, splashing another burst of water over my face and neck. Despite the fear, despite the confusion and curiosity and anxiety, I was still hard and horny as hell.

Damn it.

I leaned over the sink and stared at myself in the mirror. Two bloodshot, tired eyes blinked back at me. I squeezed my eyes shut. Shook my head. Opened them again. Same bathroom. Same me.

I let out a breath and ran through my options. Whatever was going on, this was *definitely* not normal. Now that I'd put a bit of distance between myself and that...thing, my thoughts were a little clearer, but not much. I didn't know how, but he was affecting my brain somehow. Had to be.

I fished out my phone to call for help, but it lit up to only a blinking 'no signal' screen. *Of course.*

Forcing out a breath through my nose, I white-knuckled the countertop and tried to talk some sense into myself. "Okay, you got this." Didn't matter that my voice was shaking and I was talking to myself alone in a bathroom in the middle of the night. "You can't wimp out your first night on the job. You need this. You've got overdue rent to pay, your mom's in a nursing home, and you're just trying to keep it together. You *can't* afford to quit now."

I pushed back off the counter and ran my wrists under the cold tap. I shook myself, took a deep breath, and wiped the sweat off my brow. The moment of sheer panic had passed, but there was just one problem: I didn't know what I was going to do next. Could I really keep doing my job knowing that *he* was in there? What if he escaped?

*What if...*my mind wandered...*he came for me again?*

"Fuck," I groaned. My balls ached. My cock throbbed. Every thought that wasn't panic was all-consuming arousal. What a combo, right?

Finally, I gritted my teeth and pulled at my fly. If this wasn't gonna go away on its own, I'd just have to deal with things myself. Normally I'd never think about jacking off at work, but tonight had been full of unusual circumstances. That, and I felt like if I didn't, I was gonna literally explode.

I pushed my pants and underwear down just far enough to reach my cock. Sure, I'd had some random boners as a teenager, but that was long past. This was more intense than any of them, and without any explanation why.

I wrapped my hand around my dick and hissed in a breath. Was it...bigger? I stared down at my shaft. Nah. That couldn't happen. I gave it a few good strokes up and down before squirting a bit of soap from the sink into my palm for lube. When I returned to my work in earnest, my mind flooded again with unbidden thoughts and sensations.

I was just trying to get off so I could focus and move on with my life. This erection was literally painful and I couldn't think of anything else. But the more I touched myself, the more I sunk into a hazy stupor, that heat and lust creeping through my body all over again.

Think of something sexy, anything sexy. Damn it, I tried to direct my thoughts, but they had a will of their own. Again and again, my mind drifted back to the strange creature I'd found in the lab. Again and again, I wondered how those tentacles might feel against my skin. Wrapped around my arms. Wrapped around my cock.

I sucked in a breath and winced at the shock of pleasure. This was totally wrong, but no one was watching, right? No one knew what I fantasized about, and I didn't have to tell anyone as long as I got the job done.

So for a moment, I let go of the resistance. I gave in to the feelings, throwing my head back and closing my eyes. I braced my other hand against the counter. My knees went weak. I pumped my cock faster, and my mental theater got more and more explicit.

Just what could he do with all ten of those tentacles? No man could do that. He could double penetrate me without an issue. No, triple penetrate. Or more. He could wrap one around each arm and leg, hold me trapped, and still have plenty left over to play. Not to mention the suckers lining each one, adding an extra sensory element to every touch...

"Shit!" I cursed and bucked against the sink as I crested in a sudden, fierce climax. Cum shot across the counters and splattered on the mirror. It stared back at me—evidence of my sin.

Of course, that wasn't the only unexpected thing I saw in the mirror.

Kairius was standing right behind me.

———

I SCRAMBLED TO COVER MYSELF, but it was too late. He'd already seen everything. Kairius watched me with a self-satisfied smirk, tilting his head to the side in a silent question. Almost as if he knew what I was thinking.

Almost as if he wanted to help.

I gripped the sink, still dazed from the intense orgasm, and took a step away from him. "How did you get out?" I whispered, even though I knew I wouldn't get an answer.

This was bad. This was really bad.

I yanked my pants up and hurried to fasten them. I had to get out of here. I had to tell someone. Call for help. *Something.*

Kairius simply stood there, pointing at the ceiling.

I followed his gesture and my mouth dropped open. The ventilation shaft hung open above us, the metal grating removed. Air whooshed down from above and tingled my skin.

"The vents," I breathed. "No way..."

I rushed to the door but Kai was faster. He blocked the exit with his huge body and each tentacle criss-crossed the door frame.

Oh, shit. I really was trapped.

But isn't that what you wanted? A little voice, the devil on my shoulder no doubt, spoke up in a small, teasing voice. *You wanted him here. You got off to the thought of him doing all those things to you...why don't you try the real thing?*

At this point, I didn't even know if it was me thinking those things, or some kind of hypnosis by the creature blocking the door. Did it matter?

I wanted him.

It wasn't even a completely sexual thing, either. That spark of inspiration hadn't died out since the moment I got here. That feeling of purpose. I was *here* for a reason, and maybe I was finally figuring out why. As much as he scared me, as much as I knew I should get out of dodge, I needed to know more.

I needed to help him, and it looked like the only way out was through.

"You were thinking of me." I didn't see his lips move, but heard the words clearly enough. He crossed his arms and gave me a self-satisfied smile. His tentacles still blocked the doorway.

"You can talk now?" That was news to me.

"I'm simply projecting my consciousness onto yours. You called out to me, and I responded. Now I am here."

I bit my lip. I mean, I *had* been thinking about him pretty hard, and I may have even grunted his name at one point, but I wasn't "calling out to him"—that was crazy!

And you know what was even more crazy? The fact that he somehow *heard me* and escaped the lab to come all the way here!

Something snapped in my mind. Suspension of disbelief could only get you so far, and this was so far out of the realm of possibility my mind started looking for any other explanation. You know what? Screw it. None of this was real. Couldn't be. Maybe I fell asleep at the desk or something.

But if it wasn't real, I told myself, *why not indulge a little?*

That's what it always came back to, didn't it?

Whether this was real or not, the solution remained the same. I needed to go with him. I needed to see what he needed to show me.

And yes, I needed to see just how talented those tentacles could be.

"Come here, Evan." I froze at the sound of his voice. I hadn't told him my name. "Let me help you."

I gulped. Even the most intense orgasm of my life did nothing to sate the burning within. Those tentacles, on the other hand, promised something out of this world…

"We'll make a deal," I breathed. "You help me. I'll help you."

"Hmm." Kairius made a show of stroking his chin, his tentacles squirming in excitement. A wide, wicked grin spread across his face. "Deal."

Ten tentacles shot toward me at once, buoying me to the door and out into the aquarium itself.

———

WHAT A SURREAL FEELING--BEING CARRIED by something so much bigger and stronger than me. For that small moment, my worries fled away. His skin was cool and smooth to the touch, the tentacles a slippery, silky ocean. They moved and swarmed constantly until I couldn't keep track of them anymore. But with him surrounding me like this, I knew one thing:

There would be no going back.

I let out a breath and relaxed into his embrace, watching the exhibits and fish glide and watch our movements from behind the glass. Kairius laid me down in one of the viewing rooms, filled with comfy cushions and a wide, floor to ceiling view of the tanks. Before I knew what was happening, my shoes slipped off. Then my socks.

His touches traveled up and down my sides, under my shirt and around my back. One even slipped under the hem of my pants, but he tore my attention away again when Kairius, the man, smothered my lips in a kiss.

I released a moan into his mouth and found him surprisingly pliant. The term 'fish lips' didn't even come to mind--this man knew what he was doing. As if reading my every desire, he started slow, then sped up, nipping at my bottom lip here and there before flicking his tongue out to taste mine.

I responded in earnest and leaned into him further. There were tentacles and light touches everywhere. Quick, suckling kisses that made my skin come alive. On my feet. On my hands. On my chest. Two of them wrapped themselves around my wrists before I could protest, spreading them wide above my head. He didn't stop kissing me. Didn't give me a chance to fight back.

He simply continued his assault on my senses, bringing me along for the ride. The air was thick and heavy with the scent of him--with every breath I pulled in more. With every breath I forgot myself.

Kairius pulled away from my lips long enough for me to get a good look at his face. His eyes glittered in the pale aquarium lighting, and there was something distinctly intimate about doing this, here in view of the aquatic collection. His scales grew sharper and more textured, protruding ever slightly from his face and neck. I longed to reach out and touch them, but two of his tentacles held me firm.

I wasn't going anywhere, and to be honest? That was just the way I wanted it.

How long had I dreamed of being taken like this? Of giving up total control to someone who knew me like the back of their hand? No man had ever pleased me. They always left me empty and wanting. But this...this was something else altogether. Without a word, he tapped into my most secret desires--the ones I'd never dared to voice aloud--and brought them into reality.

"Is this what you were thinking of?" Kairius' voice echoed in my mind. "When you think of me?" He dipped his head to the crook between my neck and shoulder. Something wet and slippery greased my skin, then a prick of pain-- I cried out and craned my head to the side. He was biting me--a tentacle monster was biting me.

I wailed and kicked, trying to find purchase on the floor. Of course, that got his attention. He bit down harder and sucked like a hungry vampire, sending two more tentacles to wrap around my legs and lift me off the ground.

Well, I could definitely say I'd never had sex in midair before.

And there were still eight tentacles left.

I panted and shook against him, my hands clawing out against my slippery restraints. Kairius moved away from my neck at last. I whimpered, knowing there'd be a wound there. When I looked out of the corner of my eye, though, my skin was smooth and bare as ever.

"How did you do that?" I panted, squirming in the undulating mass of slime and suckers.

"I told you," the response came just as easily. "I know what you like."

My entire body shuddered as one tentacle and then another slithered under my shirt and around my nipples. "That...you do."

How did something so foreign and so animalistic know my body so perfectly? How did those perfect little suckers know just the right places to cup my skin and leave me wanting more? I arched my back and moaned again, his work on my nipples driving me near the brink once more.

"We're not even at the main event yet..." came a teasing voice in my head.

And if he really was working off my fantasies, I knew just what that would be.

Kairius bent his head to capture me in a kiss again, but this time I felt a sudden cool air against my skin. Two of the remaining tentacles slithered under my shirt and lifted it up. He loosened his hold on my wrists just long enough to slip it off and bare my chest to him. Next was the pants--the ones he'd caught me with around my ankles in the bathroom.

I'd sloppily fastened them back together in my haste, so they didn't take much work to get back off. His lips didn't leave mine the entire time. All at once there was something playing with my hair, stroking my sides, squeezing my nipples and binding my hands and feet. How could one person do all this at once?

Correction: one *person* couldn't, but Kairius could.

I lay there, completely bare and exposed to this alien creature, stretched and spread eagled and completely at his mercy. Had someone told me this was what my first night of work would be like, I'd have laughed in their face. But here I was, suspended in midair while the most multi-talented lover in the world focused only on me.

It was shaping up to be one of the best nights of my life.

It was so hard to keep track of all the touches and sensations at once that I almost missed it when one slipped around to my backside and prodded me there. I hissed in a breath and held it while my stomach did flip flops.

Here we were, at the ultimate decision, and a last minute of fear spiked up. What if I couldn't take him? What if he hurt me? Thought after thought ran through my mind on loop, but I needn't have worried.

Kairius knew all about that, too.

"I will not hurt you," he promised me in such dulcet tones I longed to believe him. "My tentacles have a natural lubricant, and you're so aroused and relaxed already...I wouldn't attempt it any other way."

One of them swiped across my crack as if to prove a point, and I felt the wetness he left behind. It made me ache for him even more, if that was possible. I rolled my head back and exposed my neck and throat to him, closing my eyes while my mouth sagged open. "Do it," I breathed in a husky moan. "Now."

"Is this is what you wanted..." Kairius' voice faded in and out at the back of my mind. My whole world narrowed to just this moment, just this second as one of those slippery tentacles probed at my tight hole. It was narrow at the tip, easy to slip in and out, but the further you went down it grew thicker and thicker, each ridge lined with those textured suckers...

I wondered just how far I could go.

Just before slipping in, he pulled my legs wider and my arms taut. I couldn't have moved if I wanted to, and it left me completely open to him. He eased in slowly, the narrow tip breaching my hole without much issue. Especially with the lubrication coating each tentacle, it made for a slippery, friction-free ride.

And what a ride it was going to be.

My eyes flew open and I moaned louder than before, my whole body tensing up as he entered me. He slithered around my rim, in and out a little bit at a time. He stretched me little by little and went in a bit deeper each time. My eyes rolled back in my head and I gave myself to the pleasure. I felt every press of the tip. Every rub of each sucker slipping in and out. Maybe it was something about the lube on his tentacles, something about the pheromones in the air, or something about this crazy hallucination. Whatever it was, it had me floating on cloud nine, and all I wanted was *more*.

I sunk into his touches bonelessly, not caring what I looked or sounded like anymore. There was no one here to judge me. The fish wouldn't tell a soul. What did I care? The next time I moaned something wet hit my tongue, sweet and salty all at once. Through the haze of tentacles pushing in and out of my ass, around my nipples, tightening against my wrists and ankles--now there was one right at the entrance to my mouth, begging me to suck it.

"Fuck..." I panted, looking up at Kairius. "In my mouth too?"

He gave a wordless nod, flicking his length inside my ass and pushing deeper than before.

"I saw your fantasy. I saw your desire. All holes must be filled."

A shiver raked down my spine. Shame. Embarrassment. But also, surprisingly, relief. Perhaps part of my problem was that I'd never been as open as I needed to be with my lovers. Or if I was, they got weirded out and left. But with Kairius, I didn't have to worry about any of that. He saw deep down to my most depraved desires, and he didn't run. He didn't judge me.

In fact, he wanted to help me. Wanted to give me what I had been craving, but too afraid to ask for all this time.

Filled. Used. *Fucked.*

I opened up and took him into my mouth. His slime coated my tongue and stretched my lips. The perfect balance of sweet, spicy, and salty, all mixed together in one intoxicating package. I slurped him up and down, digging my tongue into each of the circular suckers in turn. He thrust gently in and out of my mouth at the same time as my ass. In and out. One, then the other. No matter what, I was always filled in one hole or the other. Who else besides a ten-tentacled monster could stroke my cock, fuck my ass, plunder my mouth, and suck my nipples all at the same time?

Oh, and don't forget the four tentacles holding me spread eagle in mid air.

That left one more tentacle unused, and at this point I had no idea where he was gonna put it...

Kairius pressed his face close to my ear, his voice a dominant force in my mind. "Is this what you wanted, Evan? To be fucked senseless in every hole? To be used like a puppet for my enjoyment?"

I whimpered, still unwilling to say it.

"Maybe this is what you needed all this time in order to find yourself, Evan. Think about it. Think about how lonely you've been."

I pushed out a breath through my nose and tried to turn my head, but his tentacle pumped faster into my mouth, deeper and deeper till it pressed against the back of my throat. I didn't want to choke, so there was only one thing to do: take him all the way.

My jaw opened wider still and I moved my tongue out of the way--Kairius did the rest. He pressed past the barrier and slithered deeper, filling my mouth to the brim.

At the same time, he picked up the pace in my ass, his thrusts rougher and deeper than before. I could feel it all the way in my belly, and I was so wrapped up I had no way to know just how deep he was. All I knew was that my ass stretched and gripped around him wider and tighter than I'd ever felt in my life. I was useless against him, a warm body and a warm hole to use and fuck to his heart's content. And fuck he did.

He slammed into my throat, he pounded into my ass, and he rocked my cock back and forth so maddeningly slow it felt like I'd been edging for days. My eyes watered and I grunted around the tentacle in my mouth, my hands wriggling and wrestling against his restraints.

Just when I thought I couldn't take it anymore, that I would die of pleasure if he didn't let me come, *please* let me come, I found out what the final tentacle was for.

It slithered out of nowhere and wrapped gently around my neck, tilting my head upward so I could look him in the eye. "That's it," he cooed. "Come for me, Evan. Come for me."

How could I resist? With a tentacle in my ass, in my mouth, around my nipples and cock and just about everywhere else, it seemed, I let go at last. My back arched, every muscle tensed for a fraction of a second, then like a spring it exploded outward, sending waves of pleasure and power rocking through me in wave after wave. I cried out, and the last thing I remembered before blacking out was the calm, serene sight of waving sea grass.

———

WHEN I WOKE, Kairius had me cradled in his arms. A warm, sleepy comfort draped over me like a blanket. I rested my head against his chest while his tentacles took turns massaging my sore muscles. I squinted my eyes open to the sight of the rising sun, cresting the horizon through the tall glass windows.

Oh man. Had I been out all night?

Despite my rigorous "activity", I felt great. Better than great, actually. I felt more awake and stronger than before. Then I had a thought.

If I was awake now, and he was still here, that meant...

Oh my god. It was real. All of it.

I covered my mouth with my hand and took a few steps backward. Kairius sensed my distress and opened his eyes, tilting his head in that strange, curious way.

"Are you leaving?" He asked.

I checked my watch. Somehow, my shift was almost over. I needed to get cleaned up and find out what to do with Kairius before Collins came back and realized anything was wrong.

He slithered over to me and placed a hand on my shoulder. We stood there for a moment, watching the sun rise. Just as he felt my concern, though, so too I felt his.

"Will you return?" He asked. It was the first time he'd sounded unsure of something.

I turned to face him. I had more than just a job as a night watchman now. We'd made a deal. If we were going to keep doing this, (and boy, did I want to), I needed to figure out more about his people. I needed to figure out where he came from. And I needed to get him out of here.

Clasping both his hands in my own, I nodded and looked to the horizon. "When the sun sets once more, I will be in your arms again."

Kairius squeezed my hand. His tentacles did their little dance. His face still looked pained and haunted, but I'd given him something to look forward to. Something for us both to look forward to.

"I'm going to get you out of here and back to your home. I promise. Don't give Collins any trouble while I'm gone, okay? We can't have him knowing about what we did."

I pulled on my clothes and tried to fix my sexed-up hair. I sighed, shrugged, and laughed. It was a lost cause.

As I left the building that morning, I couldn't help but think this job wasn't so bad after all.

It had some interesting perks, that was for certain. The benefits were pretty sweet. And I couldn't wait to go back.

———

AUTHOR'S NOTE

Thank you, reader, for picking up this book. I didn't think I would ever write a tentacle book for the longest time, even though it's been one of my favorite tropes/fetishes for years.

I thought it would be too weird. Too slimy. Too out there for most readers to enjoy.

Imagine my surprise when it became one of the most requested stories in my catalog!

Monsters are certainly having their day. There's all kinds of weird stuff out there now that I never saw a couple of years ago. They're coming out of the 'closet' so to speak, and I couldn't be happier. I get to share stories that I love with deliciously naughty readers like you.

So often in our lives we're told to stick to the path of what everyone else is doing. To stay away from those seemingly crazy ideas. This tentacle book was one of those crazy ideas, and I'm thrilled to see it actually come to fruition.

It reminds me of how I always wanted to be a writer growing up. At that time, self publishing wasn't really a thing and only a handful of people were ever 'published' — and that was after finding an agent, waiting years, and only then making a pittance. Everyone said you had to get your feet wet by submitting stories to magazines or anthologies, and maybe, possibly, if you were good enough, someone would 'notice' you. Yeah. Miss me with that. Not the best career path — or so said my parents.

So it's no surprise that I chose to study something they said would 'be a better career' in college. Four years and one computer science degree later, I still had a burning urge to write stories.

I started on the train to and from work. Little things at first, then longer and longer stories. When I got up the courage to self publish my first book in 2011, I had no idea what to expect.

No, I didn't shoot to immediate fame and fortune. It wouldn't be much of a story if I did, right?

But I learned from that one little story that there were people out there willing to pay money — real, cold hard cash — for something I wrote.

I was officially a paid author.

And what can I say? I got hooked. I wrote more things. I learned more about the business. I wrote under different pen names and floundered and failed more times than I'd like to admit.

But at the end of the day, it always came back to that dream: to write stories about the weird, dark, lustful side of myself that I kept hidden from everyone.

And finally, eventually, it took form in the story you see today.

But that's enough about me — I want to talk more about this story in particular.

I first saw The Shape Of Water on an airplane. I was actually snooping on the person's screen in front of mine. They had their headphones in, so I couldn't hear what was going on, but I could see it.

And boy, did it catch my eye.

So many romance novels and movies have a movie-star-perfect male lead for the love interest. He's there for charm and sex appeal, and it works. Those type of stories make millions each year.

But this was different. Here were two people who were by no stretch of the imagination your typical romance hero/heroines, but they found solace in one another. They connected in a way that was deeper than words, and I remember stepping off that plane with a heavy heart and thinking, "Maybe I could try something like that, too."

I still played it safe for a little while. I wrote some werewolves and dragons (I LOVE dragons) and finally I got up the courage to write the book you're reading right now. Little did I know that this book would not only delight my readers but give me confidence that I can write things I love and find readers that love them just as much as I do.

Don't be afraid to let your freak flag shine once in a while. After all, that's why you're here: because you're just as weird and freaky as I am. Welcome to the club.

So thanks for being here. Thanks for walking on the wild side with me, and I can't wait to share more naughty stories with you.

If you enjoyed reading this, there's more where that came from.

I might end up writing a sequel to this story. Who knows, it seems like Kairius and Evan have more shenanigans in store, don't you think? What if someone finds out about them? What if Kairius brings Evan to his home and learns more about the secrets of Atlantis?

And if tentacles are on the metaphorical table, why not other monsters as well? Shadow monsters. Demons. Incubi. Fae. Vampires. Spirits. Werewolves. Centaurs. Aliens. Dragons.

And of course, more tentacles ;)

That and more can be yours when you follow my author page for updates.

I hope that I'll see you around. Stay weird!

A free tale from the world of Nox Bay is all yours!

Felix, formerly a professional thief, is adjusting to his new life in pack lands. But when he receives a mysterious riddle and his mate goes missing, Felix must use his skills once more. Join him and the rest of your Nox Bay friends as he uncovers new treasures, new locations, and at the end of it all, a sweet moment with his forever mate.

https://dl.bookfunnel.com/pey6sio1dd

Join my Facebook group Connor's Coven for live streams, giveaways, and sneak peeks. It's the most fun you can have without being arrested ;)

https://www.facebook.com/groups/connorscoven/